What Can I Dream About?

by Arnold Shapiro
Illustrated by Pat Paris

PRICE/STERN/SLOAN
Publishers, Inc., Los Angeles

To Larry, Kenny, Danny and Deborah . . .

. . . may you always dream about happy things.

Published by Price/Stern/Sloan Publishers, Inc.
360 North La Cienega Boulevard, Los Angeles, California 90048

ISBN: 0-8431-4701-6

“What can I dream about?” Deborah said,
As her mother kissed her and tucked her in bed.

"Dream about happy things," her mother replied,
"Like puppies, kittens or a ferris wheel ride."

"But what if I dream of a fire-breathing dragon?"

“Then dream that he’s pulling you
in your wagon.”

"What if I dream of a monster, dirty and mean?"

“Then give him a bath so he’ll be nice and clean.”

“What if I dream a giant wants to eat me for dinner?”

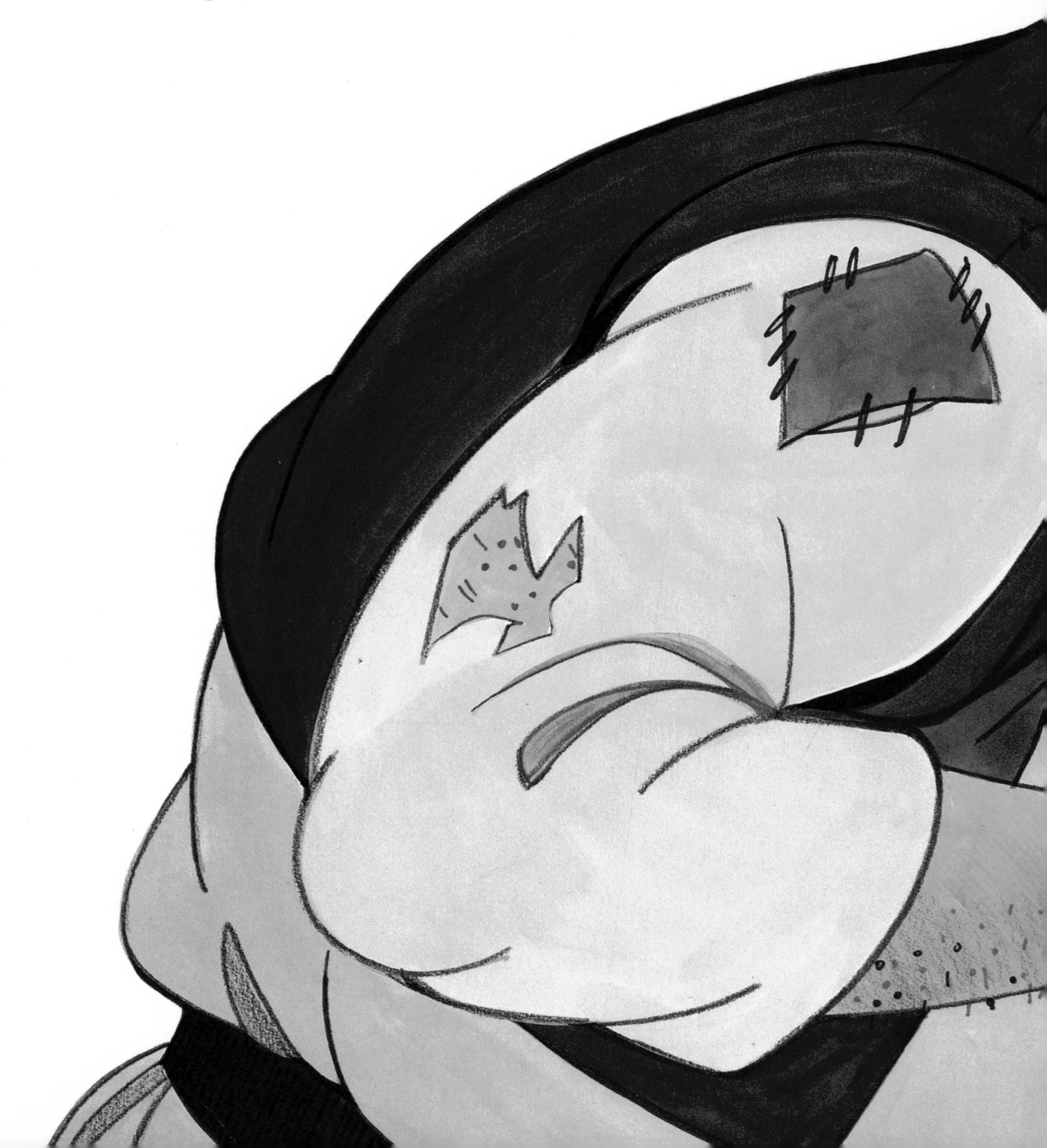

“Tell him he’s too fat
and should try to be thinner.”

“What if I dream a fierce lion is loose?”

"Dream that you tame him
with cookies and juice."

"What if I dream a pirate wants to tie me to his ship?"

“Say he has to ask me before you go on a trip.”

"What if I dream of a goblin or ghost?"

“Then dream it’s a costume party,
with you as the host.”

if I dream of a hole, dark and creepy?"
rah said with a yawn,
a he got very sleepy.

"Instead you can dream of rainbows and
Sliding on slides and swinging on swings,

Carriages, castles and jolly old kings,
The sunny, the funny, the most happy things."